REMY AND RUBY'S
RESCUE RAN
A BIG Problem
Duffield
Illustrated by
Hazel Quintanilla
Rourke Educational Media
A Division of
Carson Dellosa Education
rourkeeducationalmedia.com

Dear Guardian/Educator,
Introduce your child to the wonderful world of reading with our leveled readers. Your growing reader will be continuously engaged as he or she is guided from one level to the next. Each level is carefully built to provide your child with the reading skills and knowledge to be a confident reader! Ultimately, we want your child to develop a love of reading.

Level 1 ***Learning to Read***
High frequency words, basic sentences, large type, labels, full color illustrations to help young readers better comprehend the text

Level 2 ***Beginning to Read Alone***
Short sentences, familiar words, simple plot, easy-to-read fonts

Level 3 ***Reading on Your Own***
Short paragraphs, easy-to-follow plots, vocabulary is increasingly challenging, exciting stories

Level 4 ***Proficient Reader***
Chapters, engaging stories, challenging vocabulary, multiple text features

Reading should be a pleasurable experience. A child who enjoys reading reads more, and a child who reads more becomes a better reader. Your child will grow with exposure to broad vocabulary and literary techniques, and will develop deeper critical thinking and comprehension skills. We are excited to be a part of your child's reading journey.

Happy reading,
Rourke Educational Media

© 2020 Rourke Educational Media

All rights reserved. No part of this book may be reproduced or utilized in any form or by any means, electronic or mechanical including photocopying, recording, or by any information storage and retrieval system without permission in writing from the publisher.

www.rourkeeducationalmedia.com

Edited by: Kim Thompson
Cover layout by: Rhea Magaro-Wallace
Interior layout by: Kathy Walsh
Cover and interior illustrations by: Hazel Quintanilla

Library of Congress PCN Data

A BIG Problem! / Katy Duffield
(Remy and Ruby's Rescue Ranch)
ISBN 978-1-73161-496-4 (hard cover)(alk. paper)
ISBN 978-1-73161-303-5 (soft cover)
ISBN 978-1-73161-601-2 (e-Book)
ISBN 978-1-73161-706-4 (ePub)
Library of Congress Control Number: 2019932400

Printed in the United States of America,
North Mankato, Minnesota

Table of Contents

Chapter One

Surprise!

"Let's get everything ready," Auntie Red says.

Remy finds the smallest feeding pan. "This will be perfect," he says.

Ruby puts an old towel in a small box. “This will make a great bed,” she says.

“I can’t believe we are getting a piglet!” Remy says.

“I bet she is a little cutie,” Ruby says.

A truck **rumbles** down the drive.

"She's here!" Remy says.

Remy and Ruby rush to the truck. They look in the front seat.

No piglet.

They look in the back seat.

No piglet.

“She’s back here,” the man says.

Ruby and Remy look in the **trailer**. They can’t believe their eyes.

“We are going to need a bigger feeding pan,” Remy says.

“And a bigger box!” Ruby adds.

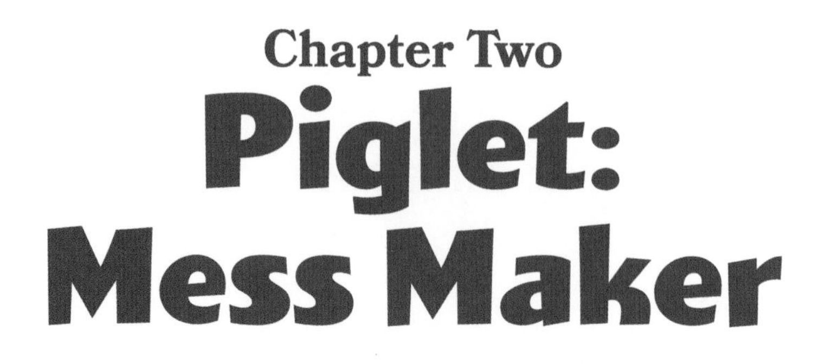

Chapter Two

Piglet: Mess Maker

“Meet Piglet,” the man says. “Piglet is a full-grown pot-bellied pig.”

“We will take good care of her,” Auntie Red says.

The family leads Piglet to the **pen**. They get her settled in.

"Let's give her some time to explore," Auntie Red says.

Later, Ruby and Remy check on Piglet. But she is not in the pen!

"Piglet!" they yell. "Where are you?"

Remy looks in the barn.

Ruby looks behind the hay **bale**.

But Piglet isn't there.

“What’s that?” Remy asks.

He points to a big hole by the fence.

“Uh-oh!” Auntie Red says. “Pigs love to dig!”

"What happened over there?" Ruby asks.

Trash covers the ground.

"Looks like Piglet has been naughty," Auntie Red says.

The family follows the trash trail.

"Found her!" Auntie Red says. "Oh, no." She points to the flower garden.

"Piglet has been *really* naughty," Remy says.

“Why did she make such a mess?” Remy asks.

“Pigs love to root,” Auntie Red says.

“Root?” Ruby asks.

“They like to push things around with their **snouts**,” Auntie Red says.

Chapter Three

One Happy Piglet

Remy fills the hole.

Ruby picks up the trash.

Remy, Ruby, and Auntie

Red replant the flowers.

"I'm tired," Remy says.

"Me, too," Ruby says.

"Uh-oh," Auntie Red says.

Piglet is busy digging another hole. A big, BIG hole.

"I think Piglet is bored," Auntie Red says. "Let's make something to keep her busy."

Auntie Red gathers some

wood, nails, and a hammer.

Tap! Tap! Tap!

Remy drags something

from the backyard.

Gurgle. Gurgle. Gurgle.

Ruby searches the toy box.

Rustle. Rustle. Rustle.

Auntie Red shows Piglet the box she made.

"It's a rooting box!" Auntie Red says.

Piglet climbs in. She root-root-roots in the hay.

Next, Remy shows Piglet the wading pool.

Piglet knows just what to do.

Splash!

Then, Ruby shows Piglet the toys.

Piglet uses her snout. She pushes the basketball. She rolls the toy truck.

"That is one happy pig," Auntie Red says.

And just like that, Piglet is not bored—not at all! In fact, she's ready for a nap. And so are Remy and Ruby!

Bonus Stuff!

Glossary

bale (bale): A bundle of something, such as hay, that is tied tightly together.

pen (pen): A small, enclosed area that holds animals.

rumbles (RUHM-buhlz): Makes a low, deep noise like the sound of thunder.

snouts (snouts): The long front parts on animals' heads, including the nose, mouth, and jaw.

trailer (TRAY-lur): A vehicle that is pulled by another vehicle, often used to carry things.

Discussion Questions

1. What are Ruby and Remy expecting when they are getting ready for Piglet's arrival?
2. Why did Piglet make so many messes?
3. Do you think you would like to take care of a BIG pig like Piglet? Why or why not?

Animal Facts: Pot-Bellied Pigs

1. Pigs are very smart animals.
2. Pigs do not smell bad! They have no body odor.
3. Pigs will eat just about anything. But they shouldn't be overfed.
4. Pigs' favorite treats include grapes, carrots, and cucumbers.
5. Pigs can be trained to do tricks such as shaking hands, rolling a ball, and blowing a horn!
6. Pigs can be trained to use a litter box.
7. Pigs have hair instead of fur.
8. Pigs cool off by rolling in mud or water.

Creativity Corner

Feeling bored isn't always a bad thing for people. Boredom can spark creativity! If there's nothing to do, you can use your imagination to come up with something new! Create a game or a puzzle about pigs that you and a friend can play the next time you are bored. Write the rules, draw a game board, and craft playing pieces from scrap materials.

About the Author

Katy Duffield is a writer who lives in Arkansas. She would truly LOVE to see a pig blow a horn!

About the Illustrator

Hazel Quintanilla loves her job, pajamas, burgers, sketch books, fluffy socks, and of course animals! Hazel had a ton of fun illustrating *Remy and Ruby's Rescue Ranch*.